CROWNING MERCY

PAUL CAMSTER

NOBEL NOMINATED AUTHOR IMPRINTS

CROWNING MERCY

PAUL CAMSTER

NOBEL NOMINATED AUTHOR IMPRINTS

CHAPTER ONE

Modesty `Modz` Pascal was tense looking out at the rows of war planes,all Sturmovics except one.It was the rocket-firing Typhoon which caught her attention-the only one without the red star emblem.Instead it had RAF roundels,She patted the documents in her pockets and sighed.Where would she be this time tomorrow?In a muddy ditch?In a POW camp?Most likely,she feared,in a large crater full of blazing airplane wreckage.
At this stage of the war,the Luftwaffe had lost control of its skies-almost.But flying low over the dwindling area still left of the Third Reich could still be lethal.She had seen an intelligence report that the person she was to seek out were themselves active in an anti-aircraft unit.Her pilot boasted of his prowess and ability to land her safely near her target,but deep down,she feared that pride came before a fall.

With the thought of the pilot in her head,he suddenly materialised,striding away from the Typhoon and waving farewell to the Soviet mechanic,who strolled away in the opposite direction.

As he entered the temporary wooden office,the

pilot asked her:"Well-got all your paperwork sorted?Got the `magic` one?"

She patted her pockets and nodded,pulling out the one he referred to as `magic`- a transparent wallet with the crest of the Soviet NKVD secret police giving her full powers in all newly-captured areas,and signed by Marshall Zhukov,commander-in chief.She liked to see the instant subservience it produced in every sentry she flourished it at,while at the same time knowing that it was her instant death warrant if she fell into enemy hands.

Glancing around the room for the last time,she passed the pilot as he held open the front door,then closed it with a click.

The airfield was unnaturally quiet as she strode towards the plane at first light,being narrowly beaten by the pilot who sprinted across to his cockpit.In a moment,he climbed in.She climbed much more carefully to the rear seat,finding the parachute pack a bulky and difficult fit.Her uniform was deliberately ambiguous.It resembled a Red Army female officers` uniform with boots and flared breeches,but her jacket and helmet was that of a pilot-of necessity,as she needed access to the radio and oxygen mask.Only the holster belt and Mauser machine-pistol stood out like a sore thumb,as it had the purpose of temporarily confusing any enemy capturing her,as she intended passing herself off as a BDM officer in the Hitler Youth for Girls on a special mission.The hope was,of course,that she would not be caught near the aircraft with its RAF markings.

The plane engine spluttered into life and it taxied away from the row of Red Air Force planes,and accelerated up the runway,rising into a sky rapidly clouding over to head west.

As they rose,plumes of smoke in the far distance denoted the active war zone and became more clearly defined through breaks in the cloud as they rose far above the lower cloud base.A crackle on their radio told her that their base was trying to communicate,and the pilot allowed her to hear the report through her headphones:"A Tiger or King Tiger tank has been reported near your intended landing zone-please seek an alternative destination....."

"Well,that`s helpful,"she rasped into the microphone."Any idea how far off-course that`ll take us?"
"No",he told her calmly,"but if the worst happens,I can take out the tank....."

"But all your under-wing rockets are fake,right?"

"Not all-two are real.The rest are fake to save weight and give us shorter take-off and landing, but our wing cannons are real.They can breach a tank`s armor in certain places....."

"From above,where it`s thinnest?"she interrupted,nervously.

"Precisely",he said,then calmly told her;"Flak-hold tight......"
Looking out,she saw tracer shells arcing up with a red glare at their tails,but the plane was evading them by a wide margin,so she breathed a sigh of relief and felt a tingle of excitement at the sight of a distant railway line with a major road running nearby.Both had nearby bomb craters from determined -but failed-efforts to cut them by dive-bombing.

She recognised their shape from the map she had studied intensively -and memorised to the point of waking up dreaming of their outlines in the shape of the terrain."It`s at the closest point where the track nears the road,"she shouted into the micro-phone.
"No need to shout-that`s where I`m heading",he snapped,then added:"see the tank-I`m going for it-hold tight."

The plane dived steeply through a break in the cloud,the tiny King Tiger growing from a pinprick to a size seeming to loom large in Modz`s imagin-ation as she felt the vibration of cannon fire leav-ing with spits of flame and sparks from its wing barrels.

The pilot had just time to shout:"It`s a fake-the shots are going thro......." before there was a shuddering jolt,followed by a rattling noise drumming loudly from the propeller and engine compartment. "We`re hit,"he shouted loudly enough for her to hear without her headphones,"I`m taking her down....."

"YOU`RE taking her down,"she told him,"looks to me like someone else`s taking us down",she yelled,almost uncontrollably.

CHAPTER TWO

As a mist of coolant trailed back from jagged holes in the engine cowling,the ground began to loom too quickly for any attempt at bailing out.Fortunately,the plane levelled out just before it reached a gap in the hedge skirting a rough field.Modz was dismayed to notice evidence of other plane wreckage strewn across the field,just as the wing tips were torn off by thick branches on either side of the gap.Modz was alarmed by being jolted forwards in her seat,but even more by the plane sliding sideways,still at high speed.Fearing the worst,she grabbed the parachute pack behind her and pushed it to the side nearest to any impact point,which was just in time as the stub of the wingtip on that side rammed into a shallow ditch, burying itself to the hilt.

Being cushioned by the pack left Modz shaken but only bruised a little on the impact side.Luckily,the canopy had been swept away by branches,allowing her to start climbing out. As there was a smell of fuel,she feared fire,but was calmer when she noticed the whole engine compartment had been torn way and was still rolling in the distance.The pilot sat still while she reached for his neck pulse, but then he started to wake up.In the distance,she could hear a hound`s voice baying excitedly,as if it had their scent.Well aware that German civilians might lynch flyers they regarded as purveyors of terror bombings,she shook the pilot awake and helped him step out of the cockpit and across the shattered wing stub to firm ground,where he became steadier on his feet.

At the gap in the hedge,an Alsation and Dobermann both appeared,with fangs bared.Realising that outrunning them was impossible,Modz reached for the pistol butt protruding from its holster,stopping only when a fearsomely stern female voice rang out:"Place your weapon on the ground and step back....."

CHAPTER THREE

Modz saw that the voice came from a female figure in Waffen SS uniform,complete with steel helmet sporting the twin lightning strokes logo.In her hand was a machine-pistol similar to that of Modz,and levelled with a steely determination that brooked no disobedience.A snap of her fingers sent the dogs heading back the way they had come.

Making the pilot and Modz turn away from looking at her,the SS woman tied both their hands behind them,then frogmarched both towards a truck hidden under some trees,and itself camouflaged with branches.She poked them both up the short step-ladder at the lowered tailgate of the truck,over which Modz noticed two nooses dangling from a tree branch.

The woman clicked the tailgate firmly in place, invited Modz and the pilot to step onto the tail-gate,then began fastening the nooses around their necks firmly,pulling a lever to release the tailgate.

As it began to fall,the executioner dragged Modz away onto the firm truck floor,but Modz was shocked to see the pilot dangling,twitching and kicking aimlessly as he swung in the air."I am Eloise Saxe-Coburg-Gotha,"she told Modz,and added: "You may call me Ele -I see you are female and not a pilot.....I wish to know who you are."

"You seem to have something against pilots,"Modz told her,as her bonds were loosened and the noose released from her neck,and added:"Why don`t you send them to a POW camp?"

"I planned to,at first-then headquarters told me they were terror flyers in international law-bandits of the air,do you see?"

"Not quite.I am BDM commander for the area," Modz told her,fumbling for the correct document from her pocket,before offering it to Eloise.

Ele examined it carefully,before pronouncing:"Impossible-I am the League of German Maidens commander for this area.....but on the other hand,it does have the signature of Reichsfuhrer Himmler...."

"Yes-and he had to put aside piles of work to sign it-you shoot planes down yourself?"Modz asked.

"Of course-I am a crack shot",Ele said,nodding towards an automatic cannon with large circular magazines,all mounted on a swivel behind the truck cab."Speaking of which,"she added,"you may have your weapon back.It is yours,I take it?"

"Yes,"Modz told her,reaching out for the Mauser machine pistol Ele had recovered and was holding out. Modz hurriedly holstered it.

Ele was clearly thinking intently before announcing:"I am going to call HQ to ask what their orders are and who is officially in command-if anyone is.Come with me....."She turned towards a covered farm wagon,and climbed its wooden steps.Inside there was an antiquated telephone,which Ele was beginning to talk into when Modz climbed the steps.The voice on the other end was just audible to Modz and she leaned closely to the handset.Ele was saying:"Yes,I understand.....let me get this straight-is that an order or a request?You wish me to report to the Horten twins` bomber and pilot it ?What if our new BDM commander here countermands that?Your order takes priority?Very well-goodbye."She hung up and turned to Modz,with a slightly annoyed look,asking her:"Your accent is slightly strange-where are you from?"

"Linz-where the Fuhrer came from,"Modz lied,then added:"but I speak ten languages,though not all to perfection...."

"That`s five more than me,then.You heard the order?"

"I take it you`ll be flying the Horten bomber?"

"Fortunately,Hanna Reitsch taught me to fly it.She was to go herself,but as you know suffered an injury test-piloting."

"Yes test-piloting can be hazardous-are you planning to take me with you?"

"Not for the final journey,no-but for the first flights you can come....."

"Er,final journey?"

"Yes,"Ele told her,"that`ll be to take the new bomb via New York.Then onward to Argentina...."

"A sizeable distance-fuel dumps have been provided en route I take it?"

"Of course-we`ll refuel in the Caribbean,where a U-boat has left a hidden cache."

"If the New York bomb is the nuclear one from Dr Werner Heisenberg`s section,will you still be welcome in Argentina?"

"The Fuhrer will,yes-he has been invited by Juan and Evita Peron.It has already been arranged to burn bodies with the dental identities of the Fuhrer and Eva Braun for the Red Army to find.Eva and their dog Blondie will reach there by U-boat...."

"Have you decided to make the first flight?"

"Yes,I`m going straight there,"Ele told her,then entered a nearby hut and barked orders.As she came away,three BDM girls-all fitting their steel helmets on- ran from the hut to take over the flak truck.

CHAPTER FOUR

As Ele strode towards her,Modz asked:"Are we being sent a scout car?To take us to the plane?"

"Not needed-it`s close enough to walk.And safer-scout cars lure dive-bombers in these parts.Follow me,"Ele beckoned with a black-gloved hand,striding down a lane heavily shaded by trees.

After a mile or so,they both heard a distant rattling noise and staccato chatter of flak shells bursting.Through the branches,Modz saw a USAF Mustang diving away from some clouds with its engine streaming smoke.Dashing to the edge of the trees,Ele was already firing her machine pistol as the plane zoomed low over an open field.Each of her shots traced a glowing arc towards the cockpit and wings,sparking brightly as they hit each until the nearest wing tank burst in a sheet of flame and the plane cartwheeled across the ground,plowing it up until the whole plane burst apart in a mushroom cloud of smoke and orange flame,from which Modz could feel a glow of heat even under the trees.

"Good shooting,"Modz told Ele,then added:"I thought I saw bits of a flying fortress near that field-was that one of yours?"

"It was,"Ele told her,"but it had already had half its engines knocked out before it came within range of me.....it was my biggest kill,though.All of its crew survived-for a while."

"I won`t ask what you did with them,"Modz said, stroking a finger across her neck.

"You have the right idea,"Ele smiled,fitting a new full magazine to her Mauser,and sliding it back into its wooden holster as she strolled on.

At length,along the left side of the country lane, Modz noticed a wire mesh fence.After a short distance,it was topped with coiled barbed wire and had the warning notices of an electrified fence.Ele turned to make sure that Modz was not too close to the fence,then waited and beckoned her to walk next to herself on the right.

They arrived at the entrance guardpost walking abreast and Ele flashed her ID document at the sentry,a BDM girl who stood to attention with steel helmet sporting an SS twin lightning strokes logo,pistol and panzerfaust. The latter was a disposable projector of a warhead capable of demolishing a tank and destroying any troops marching behind it. Ele exchanged a quick"Heil Hitler"with the sentry,and Modz did likewise,jauntily.

As they entered the huge hangar-like cavern hewn from solid rock,two boiler-suited women in stout workboots and swastika armbands approached them as the cavern echoed to the strains of Germanic marching music.

The two BDM aircraft engineers greeted Ele enthusiastically, telling her that the bat-like swept-winged aircraft mounted on its turntable with twin jet engines set into its wing-tops was ready to be taken out,and inviting Ele to try the controls.The practice bomb was fitted,they added,and could be dropped at the Atlantic target position.

As the engineers parted with a `Heil Hitler`salute,Ele stepped towards the underbelly cockpit hatch,beckoning Modz to follow.Inside the cramped cockpit,the two sat side-by side,but Modz`s side lacked any controls.Modz asked :"Can I be co-pilot,or is it impossible?"

"Impossible,"Ele told her,flicking switches and watching the dancing indicator needles.She added:"this is all a prototype,thrown together at the last minute-if it goes into production,it will have dual controls...are you ready for take-off?"

CHAPTER FIVE

"Ready",Modz told her,fastening the seat belt as the turntable rotated their view towards a seemingly solid steel panel,which then began to open.

As soon as it had slid fully back into the rock face,the plane began to roll on a gentle slope into what seemed to be a dark tunnel.

As Modz`s eyes adjusted,she could see that the roof had dim lighting.and in the distance,the tunnel ended in daylight.As Ele flicked more switches and pulled levers,the unfamiliar whine of jet engines began to build,bringing the tunnel entrance closer.At last,they reached it,and were already at near take-off speed.As Ele pulled back levers,the nose rose towards the sky,taking them at a very steep angle upwards towards the clouds. Looking down through the cockpit window,Modz was amazed to see that the ground was a patchwork of tiny fields disappearing below the clouds.

"I suppose we`re moving too fast for the enemy to catch us,but not for their radar to detect us?"Modz asked,nervously.

"They can`t catch us,no-but they can`t detect us much. We`re mostly glued wood sheeting,and the shape gives us the radar signature of a large bird....there`s almost nothing to chase.I`m going to put her on auto-pilot shortly,"Ele announced,triumphantly.

"I was hoping there`d be a gadget like that-it`s like the one in the V1 flying bombs,yes?"

"Yes-exactly like that-there was one in the V1 that Hanna Reitsch test-flew.Like this one,the V1 cockpit was a last-minute makeshift and most male pilots were too big and clumsy to fly it. Several were killed trying.....but why are you glad about it?"

"I have something to show you where there`s no danger of interruption and where you`d be perfectly relaxed."

Ele adjusted her seat back angle to a more relaxed position,watched Modz fumbling in her jacket pockets and told her:"That sounds intriguing-are you ready to show me now?"

"Yes",Modz told her nervously,holding out two certificates,one yellowing and one crisply fresh.

CHAPTER SIX

"Birth and death certificates,yes?I don`t understand-what have they to do with me?"

"You`ll see that your birth certificate names your..."

"Father-as George Saxe-Coburg-Gotha,King of England,"Ele whistled and took a deep breath.

"Even better,"Modz told her eagerly,"he`d married your mother before the Bowes-Lyon woman,without getting a divorce......"

"So he`d committed bigamy?"Ele asked,nonplussed.
"What`s that mean?"

"The later marriage was illegitimate,along with any offspring...."Modz told her,carefully studying her reaction.

Thinking intensely,Ele flourished both certificates,then concluded:"Does that mean I`m the legitimate heir-but only if he dies.....?"

"Oh,he`s dead alright-that`s his death certificate you`re holding."

Ele carefully examined the newest certificate she was holding."It says he died in an asylum-so who was ruling....er,reigning?"

"That would be a lookalike stand-in.He lost his mind in a Satanic cult ritual-naturally,it had to be kept secret."

"I`ll bet it did,"Ele sighed."I never knew him-I was brought up by foster parents and governesses..... What do you propose to do about this?"

"I aim to take you back to claim your throne,Majesty."

"They`ll never accept me in this uniform,"Ele gestured with a hand towards her whole uniform.

"Then we`ll have to change it for you-what`s that little red light flashing?Just there...."Modz pointed ,at the control panel.

"It means we`re near the target area-we go back to manual control.I`m going to take her below the cloud base or we`ll miss the target....."

"Is it near that shipwreck?"Modz asked,staring down through the cabin side windshield.

"Very close,"Ele told her,sighting the target through a small screen with circular lines and a cross hair reticule at the center. Grabbing the bomb release button on its ball -jointed mount,she counted quietly down:"Three,Two,One......Gone!"At that,the plane jolted upwards with the speed of an elevator with its dead weight tonnage gone,and after a brief sigh of relief,she announced:"The bomb camera will follow it down by its smoke trail. When it hits,it will leave a puff of smoke-there-see it?"

"Not a very big bang,then-compared with the New York bomb....."

"No,"Ele told her"We won`t need that accuracy either-and we`ll have to fly higher.It`ll go off far above the skyscrapers and vaporize everything for two or three miles around. The radiation will make the place uninhabitable for two millenia.....I`m taking her down now to refuel.Seat belt on tight?"

Modz nodded as they swooped low over a small island surrounded by white surf in the vastness of the blue ocean.In what seemed liked moments,they were swooping low,then the jet whine started to die down as Ele lowered the wheels and touched them against a smooth strip alongside the beach.Modz lurched forward in her seat as the brakes bit and the jets died.Eager to see where they were,she lowered the hatch and climbed down the lightweight steps onto sandy soil,glad to breathe the clean air with its salt spray from the surf, totally free of the burning aircraft smoke she had endured for days.She watched as Ele lifted a camouflaged lid near the plane,and paid out a deep

green hose pipe,taking its metal spout over to the plane`s refuelling cap under a streamlined flap.
A buzzing pump and a rhythmic wiggle in the loops of hose lying on the ground told her the fuel was flowing briskly,as did the smile on Ele`s face.

Examining another camouflaged lid,Modz was amazed to find that it had all kinds of provisions,from drinking water to all kinds of tinned and preserved food and wines of every variety. Excitedly,she called to Ele,who was just returning the fuel hose to its reel:"We could live here for a year on this-or until the war`s over....."

Ele smiled then told her:"Living like Swiss Family Robinson on a desert island has its attractions, but my BDM girls need me-lazy as they are-they won`t survive without me. Then there`s my new reign...."

"They`ll all manage without you-for a while.I`ve got documentation which will get us through enemy lines when the time comes.You could fly straight to London-the English would be ever so grateful for a plane like this-they might even crown you on the spot...."

"Yes-with a sledgehammer,"Ele laughed,then added:"if my dad was a maniac Satanic cult leader,isn`t that a job I`ll have to take on?"

"At least have a drink and a think on it,"Modz told her,flourishing a bottle of champagne and two paper cups she`d pulled from the supply dump,

Ele looked at her with an angry glance,telling her:"You want me to fly us back plastered?Some of that is for the Fuhrer to celebrate when we destroy New York,"then noticing that Modz had already began pouring the bottle,added:"you`ll have to finish the bottle now it`s open-it`s too expensive to waste...."She turned her back on Modz who was guzzling the champagne with gusto,and headed to the cockpit hatch,beginning to climb its steps and shouting back:"come on,if you`re coming-or Ill go without you...."

CHAPTER SEVEN

Modz was already beginning to buckle at the knees when she reached the the steps,and could barely climb into the hatch carrying the bottle in one hand and two paper cups overflowing with fizz in the other.She pushed down the hatch cover and slumped into her seat next to Ele,guzzling the cup contents and shoving the cork roughly into the bottle opening.She barely heard the jets whining as they powered up and the plane turned into the wind before hurtling down the short runway and climbing at a steep angle across the white surf spray and blue ocean.

As they approached Germany,Ele was troubled by the blue smoke haze rising from the populated areas between the green patchwork expanse of forest and farmland. Denser blue plumes,sometimes with flecks of thick yellow signalled fires from air raids.Angered by this,Ele was almost elated at the sight of a flying fortress and its Mustang fighter escort lumbering at what seemed a slow pace at a low altitude compared with her height and speed.She was gratified to find that the cannons hastily fitted to the Horten jet were fully charged with ample shells.

Making a half-turn,Ele began to dive towards the pair,and the Mustang peeled away from the bomber to take her on.She could hear his frantic shouts on the radio,screaming to the bomber pilot to ditch the weight of his bombs,an order he seemed to ignore.She noticed the Mustang trying to climb with its nosed raised enough to fire at the jet,diving from far above,and as he loomed within her cross-hairs,she squeezed the button in her gloved hand,rattling off a stream of cannon shells with the bright glow of a tracer flare at the base of each one.The stream caught the Mustang cockpit and wing root,blowing both apart. Satisfied,she slowed up her in her dive,as the flying fortress lumbered so slowly compared to her speed as to seem almost stationary.A couple of wildly inaccurate streams of tracers left a smoke and spark trail from the fortresses ` gun turrets,but they missed her jet by a huge margin,as the gunners clearly underestimated her speed.Bringing them swiftly into her cross-hairs,Ele rattled off a stream of cannon fire,bursting one gun turret apart,with its munitions firing off bright glowing embers at high speed,glittering even in daylight.Although smoke was trailing from the fortress,Ele was about to ensure its demise with another stream of shells,when a wing root split,pouring out a sheet of bright orange flame longer than the fortress itself.She hastily pulled back the stick to climb steeply, banking away from the fortress just as its bomb load detonated,rattling her instrument panel and sending chunks of smoking debris in every direction,some only narrowly missing the Horten jet as it regained its ceiling.

CHAPTER EIGHT

Modz began to rouse from sleep with a groan,just as she slumped forward against her seat belt from the plane diving and slowing as its base runway loomed in the distance,with Ele skidding its lowered landing gear on the narrow runway between forests of trees,cutting the jets to zero and braking intensely enough to raise blue tyre smoke as the plane raced into the base tunnel with its wheel squealing to a halt -helped by an arrester cable- a few meters from the steel door,which slid open.

The engineer in her boiler suit but without its swastika armband dashed into the tunnel,attached a winch hook to the plane undercarriage,and began winching it onto the turntable. As soon as it clipped into position,Ele rose from her seat,gave Modz a shake on the shoulder to fully wake her, and beckoned her to follow,lifting the hatch and climbing down the steps.The engineer asked how did it all go.

"Extremely,well,"Ele told her,"you `ll find the bomb camera footage in its cartridge-it sounded as if it filmed everything needed...."

"That`s good,"the engineer replied,"but there`s bad news here-the Reds have broken through.Our sentry and and one of your BDM anti-aircraft girls are trying to slow them up down the lane,but it might only be a matter of time...."

"I left three BDM girls with that gun-Lena,Nena and Margret-I`ll have to check on them....."Ele began to break away towards the front exit when the enginerr waved her back,and pointed to Modz, who was rushing to catch her,but with a slightly staggering gait.

"One more thing",the engineer called out,and waited to be sure that Ele and Modz were listening before telling them:"As soon as you leave,I`ll be setting the timer....."

"Timer?" Ele and Modz both called out simultaneously.

"The one to blow the entrance and exit tunnels,"the engineer told them,then went on:"they can`t deliver the atom bomb now-they did think of sending it with a Japanese pilot who offered to deliver it to the enemy kamikaze style,but even that is too late.Before you go,you should take some of these....."She held out slings containing three or four panzerfaust disposable tank-killers with shaped charge warheads.They each grabbed a bundle and slung them over their shoulders,as they headed for the exit.The engineer followed them and flicked a switch under a locked flap as she exited,and hidden clockwork began to whirr.

Down the lane,Ele spotted a familiar shape under some trees near the old rural churchyard.Behind her,the engineer and her assistant crossed the lane and headed across a field,looking for tanks with their panzerfausts.

As Ele and Modz neared the anti-aircraft truck under its sheltering trees,they saw three hunched figures standing on the horizontally locked tailboard of the truck.All three were hooded,and as she got closer.Ele saw three nooses-all with professional-looking spiral knots- being adjusted on a long overhead branch by Lena,stretching up on her booted tip-toes.

"All three flyers?"Ele called out.

"Yes-Heil Hitler",Lena called back,and added:"you may want to interrogate the middle one-I don`t know enough English."

"Why only the middle one?"

"He killed Nena-and your two dogs......"

"My beautiful dogs?Gone?"Ele had to stop herself from sobbing,then walked across and climbed the truck steps firmly,then pulling off the hood of the middle man,whose hands were tied,like the others-behind his back."No-please,"he mumbled," just shoot me if I`ve got to die...."

CHAPTER NINE

"You`d be drawn and quartered if I had my way,"Ele told him,stretching up to fix the noose tightly,and adjusting it upwards until he was on tip-toes,and barely breathing before pushing him writhing and twitching off the tailboard.She left the other two hooded,slipped the nooses over the hoods to their necks,tightened them and pulled the lever to release the tailboard,so that all three swung kicking and moaning in a stifled way under the creaking and groaning branch.

"You can see Nena buried if you like,"Lena called out,and pointed across the lane to the old churchyard,just as a series of blasts almost threw them to the ground. Hearing the direction and muffled nature of the blasts,Ele stood upright and rushed to steady Lena on her feet."No need to worry-it`s the tunnel demolition timer",Ele told her,then asked: "did you have a near-miss when Nena died?"

Lena nodded,and choked up,putting a crumpled handkerchief to her nose and blowing it,after wiping away a stream of tears she breathed deeply,then told Ele:"The flyer was hanging in a tree by his parachute harness,his feet knee height above the ground.Nena rushed forward with the dogs,and he shot all three.Only when Margret rushed up with a panzerfaust and threatened to blow him apart did he drop his pistol and release his harness.....”

“He`s got a different kind of harness-better suited now,”Ele told her,patting her on the shoulder as they resumed the path into the church lych-gate with Modz and Margret running to join them.

Gathered around the ancient crypt containing Nena`s ancestors-all listed in stone on the outside-they all muttered a swift `goodbye` to Nena,who was lying with arms crossed in an open coffin in her cream long woollen underwear with ribbed cuffs at the wrists and ankles,under dark boot socks.Afterwards,Lena and Margret placed the lid on and tapped down the raised panel pins already lightly tapped in around the edges.Lifting the coffin,they were helped by Ele and Modz,who light-ened the load as they entered the crypt and slid the casket onto a shelf already marked`Nena`.Ele was shocked by the dates engraved that showed her age to be not quite fifteen.On the shelf opposite,Ele saw her two dogs,respectfully arranged,and fought the tears which began to flow.Her melancholy got even worse when the strains of a hymn began to play,first in English,then German.It was `The Day Thou Gavest Lord Is Ended`.It was a slightly scratchy recording,gotten -Margret later told her-fromthe portable service pack of an RAF chaplain

who was found parachuted into a tree with his neck broken.

CHAPTER TEN

As the music died,and Lena closed the crypt door,Margret recited the words:"Holy Mary,blessed art thou among women,be with us all now and at the hour of our death......Amen..."As they broke away,each of them was mopping tears from their eyes with their handkerchiefs.

As Margret and Lena returned to their anti-aircraft truck,Ele and Modz said a swift goodbye and made their way up the lane in the direction the Red Army tanks were expected. A boom in the distance told them that the engineers had blown as many road bridges as they could to delay things,but a distant mechanical clatter,so far away it was almost a tinkle,was getting gradually louder.Two or three recognizable thuds followed by louder booms told Modz that panzerfausts had been launched from their blackpowder tubes and exploded against tank armour.Plumes of smoke rising to the clouds in the distance told her that the tank crews had been cremated by the focussed metal cone which formed a hypersonic jet cutting clean through the sturdiest tank.

As they rounded a high hedge-topped bend in the

lane,a fearful and frightening sight met them.A T34 tank with the red star insignia was halted a few hundred meters away.Behind it,as far away again,was a set of T34s burning.Some were exploding their munitions like a fireworks display.The nearest tank had its commander directing a stream of machine-gun fire againt the attackers,at a location Modz could not see.She motioned to Ele to remove her swastika armband,and quickly did the same,dropping both into the hedge.As they both had sweaters,jodhpurs and boots,they could pass as Soviet troops from a distance.Modz quickly removed her sling of panzerfausts and helped Ele do the same,carefully concealing both bundles in the undergrowth.Ele became agitated and asked her:"Are you crazy-now we`re almost unarmed......"

"Not quite,"Modz told her,and pulled out a hammer and sickle flag,holding it out in front of her as she approached the tank,with Ele following nervously.

The tank commander-who Modz was hugely relieved to see was female-leaned out of her turret as Modz held out her NKVD commander credentials,and they saluted each other.The commander shouted nervously:"Seen any BDM or Hitler Youth vermin,comrades?"

"No,why?"Modz asked innocently.

"I`ve lost a dozen tank crews this morning-we`ve nailed some of the pests,but there was one behind every tree back there.I`d like to get my hands on them......"

"So would I-those girls need spanking-I blame the parents."Hiding her face behind Modz,Ele snorted as she tried to stifle laughter.

"We need a ride to the British sector,"Modz told the tank commander,"have you any transport?It`s top priority."

"There`s just the top of the tank-I`m going that way-who`s you friend?"

"She`s an NKVD dog handler....."

"Where are the dogs."

"We were hunting for BDM and Hitler Youth-there was shooting and they ran off",Modz told her.

"Too bad-maybe you`ll spot them from the back of the tank-I`m Anna-what`s your name?"

"Er,Modesta,but everyone calls me Modz."

"Well,climb up Moza.You`ll be glad to know that it`s safer up there than marching behind.I`ve lost countless troops marching behind their tanks,but none on top."

"Glad to hear it,"Modz told her,climbing up and hauling up Ele after her,as the tank gradually edged forward.

As they were going back the way Ele and Modz had

come,they approached the churchyard and Anna stuck her head out of the turret hatch,cheerfully calling:"Both comfortable I hope-I`ve just radioed our military police to be on the alert-had to shoot one of my best men at the last cemetary.Caught him trying to steal jewellery buried with the deceased,Ever had to do that?"

Ele was about to shake her head when Modz piped up:"Not personally,but my dog-handler here has had to do executions....For similar offenses,you understand..."

"Oh you poor thing,"Anna told Ele."the one I shot",she went on,"had unearthed a young lady freshly buried and was about to......You know...."

"Disgusting",Modz told her,"you were right to shoot him on the spot-I would have done."

"The solemn duty of us in high command,I guess.Do you need ear muffs?I have some if the engine noise bothers you.We`re making a cautious pace until our air-recon photos come in.The Sturmovics are taking out any tanks in our path.If we have to speed up I`ll give you muffs for the extra noise."

"Thanks,"Modz told her,and she disappeared into the hatch.

They soon passed the anti-aircraft truck,and Modz drew a sigh of relief as they clattered past the well-hidden truck and she noticed no hanging bodies, but Lena and Margret hiding below the truck with panzerfausts. Fortunately,she noticed that both of them recognised her,and she gave them a sly wave,as did Ele.They gave a sly wave back,and held their fire.

At the sight of rubble across the lane,Anna popped up her head from the hatch and told them:"Hold tight-we may rock and roll over this bomb crater -looks like an ammo dump went up-what do you think?"

"I think the same," Modz told her,as the tank tilted sideways,sliding a little from passing over the spot where the lane sloped sideways from the tunnel blasts.

"Good news"-Anna shouted above the loud clatter and rumble as the rock split and crushed under their tracks.She held one earpiece of her headphones on over one ear and continued to shout:"the British have just cleared some mines and laid a pontoon bridge across the Elbe-they`ve told us we`ll be able to cross."

"Glory Alleluia,"Modz sighed,too quietly for Anna`s ears,as the loudest crunching of the tank tracks on rubble eased off past the tunnel blast site.

After a long bone-rattling drive along the lane,Anna`s tank at last swung onto some soft ground between trees and hedges,making slower progress,but to Modz`s way of thinking a much more comfortable and quieter one.The glimmer of a distant river in fading sunlight told her that the Elbe crossing was within reach.

As they reached the pontoon bridge along a track with the German `Achtung Minen`notices pasted over in English with `Mines Cleared`,two khaki-clad sentries approached Anna`s tank.They saluted and called to her in Russian as she popped her head up,and she saluted back:"Sorry Major-the bridge won`t take the tonnage of your tank-we`ll ring for a jeep to take you across-who do you want to see?"

"I don`t want to see anybody,"Anna told them,"but my passengers want to see Field-Marshal Montgimery."

"Do they now,"the sergeant replied,"and what might be the business they want to discuss with him if you please,Major?"

CHAPTER ELEVEN

Modz jumped down and helped Ele climb down after her.

Ele followed unsteadily after being cramped on a rattling metal platform,as Modz pulled out a document showing that she was commander of the SO-E,and thrust it towards the sergeant.

The sergeant examined it on both sides before concluding:"Special Operations Executive?I`ve certainly heard of them-you`ll be wanting to discuss top secret material I suppose?What about your friend?"

"She`s our dog-handler,"Modz told him,with a straight face,as Ele tried to hide a smirk behind her back.

"Where`s her dog?",the sergeant asked.

"That`s one of the secrets we can only discuss with General Montgomery,"Modz told him,as Anna shouted across "I`ve just had a a radio instruction to be somewhere else-I`ll be saying good-bye....."She saluted and then waved as her tank engine roared into life and the tank swung around back the way it came,with its tracks flinging clods of earth high into the air as it speeded up.Modz and the sergeant both saluted and shouted goodbye,but Modz had to step hastily in front of Ele to hide her wave,which too closely resembled the Hitler salute for comfort.

"My corporal`s phoned for a jeep,"the sergeant told them,"there-it`s just coming now,See it?"

As they stared across the glimmering water,in the gathering gloom,Ele saw the jeep`s lights glitter off the sides of the pontoon bridge,with a bow wave rippling out in all directions as the jeep`s weight pushed down on each boat the wooden plank road passed over.

Modz and Ele hurriedly climbed into the back seats as soon as the jeep arrived,both anxious for a comfortable and restful ride at last.Even the stream of tracer bullets from further up the east bank pinging off the pontoons like fireflies as they they raced across to the West side failed to trouble them much.The tracers stopped as a stream of counter-fire from the West bank streaked across."Hitler Youth and BDM hooligans",the driver told them,"I shouldn`t let it bother you."

"We don`t",Modz told him,"I think they need spanking-I blame the parents.....",she yawned,then went into a deep sleep,slumping against Ele,who was already fast asleep.

They only awoke at the sound of a deep,guttural voice asking the driver:"Who are these two sleeping beauties?"

Modz woke first,and thrust her SOE credentials in the direction of the guttural voice.The military policeman in a cap with a red hat-band,which Modz could just make out from the light of his torch,proceeded to examine both sides of her document in the torch beam,then handed it back and saluted, which Modz could just see as the gloom was broken by first light.The pole across the road between sentry boxes was raised as the jeep rored through.

The driver screeched to a halt near a temporary wooden map-room which had a figure standing in the doorway in low light.Modz was just able to recognize him as Montgomery,whom she had only seen on newsreels.As she climbed out of the jeep and approached,closely followed by Ele,he told them both:"As you`re SOE,we`ve got one of yours who`ll guide you home to your London HQ.She`s in the next map room....."He pointed to a wooden map room a few meters away,just as its door was opening."Have a pleasant trip,"he told them,then saluted and turned back to his map-table.

The outline of a young woman in even dimmer light called to them both in a very posh accent:"I`m Odette-I have your air tickets.I`ll be going with you."She marched up to them in brisk military style and handed each a ticket."My jeep`s at the back of the hut,if you`d care to step this way",Odette told them and stepped briskly between the huts,as they followed.She ensured that each was comfortably seated before climbing into the driving seat and racing off with a spin of the rear wheels raising a plume of dust trailing behind them.

Odette drove at extraordinary speed through the winding country lanes,slowing down only to squeeze past wide military vehicles coming the other way.Soon they were at a wide airfield with a long runway and were driven up to a light plane just large enough for three.Odette helped Modz and Ele into the rear seat,and told them:"I see you`re dressed for flying-very sensible.I hope they gave you nice warm underwear-one can`t be too careful."

Both nodded quietly and Modz told her:"I hope you are too."Ele noticed that the plane was a German spotter plane called a Stork or `Storch`but with its German cross markings replaced with RAF roundels.

They relaxed a little as the single propeller powered up and Odette began to taxi down the runway.The short take-off length told them why the Stork had been chosen,and it rapidly reached above cloud height.They each put on oxygen masks at Odette`s bidding,as it lacked the luxury of the Horten jet,having no pressurized cabin.

They also felt a chill from the altitude,but were able to admire the countryside of Western Germany,then France until the English Channel glimmered in the distance.

C HAPTER TWELVE

Crossing the south of England ,they could already see London looming under a thin bluish smoke haze,and were alarmed to notice that Odette was descending over the capital.As she approached Buckingham palace,having already circled it,Ele grabbed Modz`s arm and squeezed it tightly."Hold tight,now,"Odette told them,and swooped in towards a long stretch of garden lawn.

Ele closed her eyes tightly and clenched her fist as the wheels squeaked on the damp grass,and they were pitched forwards as the plane decelerated hard,squealing to a halt a few meters from a grove of fruit trees.

A guard rushed out from somewhere,clutching a rifle and bayonet until he saw Odette`s pass which she thrust out of the open cabin door.Modz did likewise with her pass and they all stood unsteadily until the guard told them to follow him and walked briskly into an entrance,where he waited with the door propped open.
Moving along a corridor,the guard opened a door, said something to someone inside,and beckoned them over then motioned for them to enter a glit-

tering room with gilded plasterwork and candela-
bras. A familiar figure sat at a large ornate desk.

CHAPTER THIRTEEN

They all recognised him as King George.Ele was open-mouthed with astonishment," But....you`re dead-your Majesty.How can it be?"

"King George is dead yes,but you`re the Majesty now,your grace,"he told her,in a voice familiar from newsreels and the radio."I`m his lookalike and stand-in. Everyone has them.Mr Hitler,Mr Stalin,General Montgomery,even Odette here...."

They all turned to look at Odette,who told them:"No,no-I`m real",she patted herself and laughed.

As he motioned for them all to sit down in soft armchairs,`George`went on:"It was in this very room that his late majesty met his downfall.One Mr Aleister Crowley-no doubt you`ve heard of him?"he looked around and saw all three nodding their heads."He arranged a ceremony to enable king George to be revenged on two women using the Order of the Garter talisman.A sacrifice was arranged in this very room to the Lord Satan-or it may have been Lucifer,I forget which....."

"You mean that actually happened?"Modz asked,"I assumed that was propaganda by Mr Goebbels."

"If only it were",he told her,"they were so successful that they invoked the terrible `Angel of Death` spirit which was turned against them by the victims.The sacrificial brazier exploded,killing most of the Satanists,and George became insane.He had to be kept in a padded cell,and died there mysteriously. This whole section of the building was burnt out and even its scorched brickwork was scattered across the lawn.It looked like a bomb had hit it-and they told everyone it had....."

"The Satanists were cremated And went to hell in the same moment?Doesn`t this room scare you-in case it all happens again?"Modz asked.

"By night,yes-I keep my distance,"he told her,and added:"Everyone is afraid to enter this wing by night."Turning to Ele he told her:"Although king George is gone,only we know of it-therefore I can remain in the post for as long as you wish-and obey your Majesty `s orders if you need time to prepare for the role......"

Ele turned in her seat to face him,and told him with a noticeable German accent:"Thank you,yes,I shall need time to prepare.I`ll need elocution lessons to get the accent right.Also,I`ve been invited by President and Evita Peron to visit Argentina...."

"You mean they know about your position?",he asked,looking astonished.

"Argentina is full of Germans-of course they know

I`m the heir,but not that my father`s dead...."

"I must say you don`t seem very upset,"he told her stiffly.

"I`ve had a long time to get used to it-and had a few narrow escapes,"she told him coldly,"and besides,I hardly knew him.He was a childhood memory and broke my mother`s heart....."Her eyes began to fill with tears,and Modz leaned over to offer her a handkerchief,while turning her head to tell him:"Her Majesty has had a tiring journey since I was sent to collect her from very dangerous circumstances."

"I`m very sorry,"he replied."I had no idea."Do you wish me to arrange your visit to Argentina shortly or in a few weeks?"

"She`ll be going shortly,"Modz told him."Arrange it as soon as you can.When we`ve had a light lunch,we`ll be going to bed to catch up on beauty sleep."

He pressed a button on his desk and a maid appeared in the doorway.He told her:"Please escort Her Majesty and her,er,lady-in waiting to their rooms and make sure they have whatever they need."

"Yes sir"the maid curtsied,and held the door for Ele and Modz to make a tired shuffle from their chairs down the corridor with her.Both were relieved to find that their rooms were not in the Satanic sacrifice wing and quickly made themselves at home in the two adjoining rooms,opening the adjoining door to whisper while awaiting the lunch trolley.

Modz asked Ele whether she thought:"The invition-do you suppose it has anything to do with the Fuhrer arriving by U-boat?"

"It has everything to do with it,"Ele told her."I hope you`ll be coming along-my Spanish is even worse than my English......"As Modz nodded,there was a knock on the door and the lunch trolley arrived.Ele pretended she had been at the dressing table near the door,brushing her hair.

As they were finishing their lunch together,Ele asked Modz whether she had heard a strange muffled screaming sound along the corridors of the wing where the Satanic ritual room they had just left was located.

Modz nodded,and added:"I didn`t want to say anything in case everyone thought I was scaremongering...."

CHAPTER FOURTEEN

Just then the housekeeper arrived to remove the lunch trolley,so Modz decided to risk asking her:"Can you tell us what became of the late King George`s family by his latest marriage,please?"Flinching,and expecting a rebuff or a well-rehearsed `official` story,Modz tried to pretend she had not asked,and Ele hid her face.

The housekeeper was unfazed as she grasped the trolley handle,telling Modz:"They were afflicted with the same condition he was afflicted with, Madam."

"You mean madness?"Modz found herself asking-scarcely able to believe she`d spoken the word.

"Just so,Madam",the housekeeper told them calmly.

"Can I visit them?where are they located?"

"Within this building,Madam.But they are far too ill to be visited.They have to be sedated at all times...."

"But is their condition curable?"Ele asked,leaning back in her chair in a shocked state.

"Not by modern medicine,Majesty.it is said that an expert at exorcism may be able to help,but so far none has been found."

"I know something of exorcism-the priest at my convent school practised it,"Ele told her,and added:"if you see the doctor,please tell him I`m willing to try."

"I will pass on that message, Majesty."The house-keeper curtsied and left with the trolley,closing the door behind her.

Modz hissed in a whispering tone in case her words were overheard:"You don`t really know how to cure them surely?It was just a word of com-fort,yes?"

"No-what do you take me for?If they can`t get any-one better,I`ll have a go-what is there to lose?"

"Only your life-or your soul,if they`re in a demon-iacally possessed state."

"Don`t worry-I won`t rush into it.According to the school exorcist,women can`t....."

"Can`t what?"

"Rush into it.He said it took a lunar month to pre-pare.They had to be a strict virgin,of course."

"Of course,"Modz smirked.

"No,you`re making fun of it-during the preparation they have to wear wool or silk next to the skin over the whole body-it has to be white,beige or ecru-that`s a kind of pale yellow.It has to cover from wrist to ankles night and day...."

"Well,you`ve done that",Modz told her,"you wore long combinations in all weathers on your anti-aircraft truck.You haven`t had time to change them,right?"

"Pretty much-you`re saying I`m ready now?"Ele asked,pulling at her cream ribbed wrist cuff under her sweater.

"That school priest or chaplain guy was probably just trying to put you off-he wanted to keep exorcism for himself.Why not call him in to help?"

"He was called in by a Gestapo head who`d got some personal demons- they`re probably both in Paraguay by now.Tell you what-let`s get their doctor in first-get his permission.Do you see?"

"With crystal clarity,"Modz told her,and handed her the telephone from the dressing table.

"You call,"Ele said,"my English isn`t good enough yet,and he won`t like the sound of my German."

Modz nodded,picked up the receiver,and asked the butler to send the doctor attending the late George`s most recent family.Hanging up,she told Ele:"He`s on his way".

The doctor knocked,and entered in his white coat.he was bearded,and sat in the chair facing them as Modz waved him towards it."Your patients",she told him calmly,"her Majesty is anxious to help them.She wants to get treatment for the demonic aspects...."

He lit a cigarette,leaned back and told her:"I wouldn`t try that,"then noticing the puzzled expression on Modz`s face.added:"it`s the most dangerous aspect.If I may make a suggestion,helping their look-alikes may be more fruitful."

"Their look....alikes?"Modz asked,completely nonplussed.

"Yes-naturally they have them,"he told her calmly,blowing a cloud of blue smoke towards the ornate ceiling before continuing:"all their newspaper and newsreel appearances feature them-it would be pointless having rabidly mouth-foaming persons screaming obscenities at the cameras...."

"Is that what they do?"

"Unfortunately yes-and it`s unlikely to change.It may even be contagious-a male nurse sedating them was afflicted with the same symptoms,but he did indicate that he was a Satanist,so he was joining his own."

"So for the foreseeable future,there can be no help?"

He shook his head and blew a smoke ring which curled up and broke on a gilded cherub fresco before adding:"None whatever-and if you`ll take my advice,you`ll take Her Majesty as far away as you can-with modern communications she can control events here in the palace from a safe distance."He stubbed out the nub end in a saucer,and lit another cigarette,even though Ele and Modz were both beginning to cough.

"Well,thank you doctor."Modz told him,searching for an excuse to get rid of him,and adding:"we`ll take your advice to the letter-and maybe we can communicate by long-distance telephone if that suits you."

"Suits me fine,"he told her,heading for the door and flicking his cigarette ash randomly en route.

"`Bye doctor,"Modz told him,almost choking from the smoke, then rushing to the window for fresh air as he closed the door behind him.

Getting back to Ele,who was coughing into a handkerchief,Modz told her:"We`d be best heading to Buenos Aires as soon as possible-will you be piloting us?We have the royal flight air pool to choose from-I`ll ring through to tell them you`re coming."

"Fine,"Ele said,rising from her seat,"I`ll get my flying helmet".She headed to the shoulder bag lying on the bed where she`d flung it,and pulled out the helmet,then headed out of the door as Modz rushed to follow.

CHAPTER FIFTEEN

They reach the King`s Flight airfield by chauffeured limousine and stepped out near a twin-engined private plane marked with royal insignia.Ele climbed the portable steps,followed by Modz,and the steps were rolled away.

As Ele climbed into the pilot seat and checked the controls,Modz climbed into the co-pilot`s seat and fitted the headphones with its microphone,as it was agreed that her English was much more fluent for the benefit of the control tower.Modz quickly got clearance for take-off and they taxied into the oncoming wind to make a short take-off.

Stopping only at a small Atlantic island airfield to refuel,they reached the airfield ordered to be cleared for them by Evita Peron,landed with fuel running low,and both fell into a deep sleep from exhaustion.At daybreak,a hamper arrived by limousine from Evita,with luxurious foodstuffs and chilled champagne,all of which they gorged as if starving.

A limousine with darkened windows arrived just as they were wiping their hands on the napkins provided,and climbing down the mobile airfield steps.As Modz stared in disbelief,a familiar figure stepped out and was greeted by Ele without hesitation:"Heil Hitler-mein Fuhrer,how was your journey,"she asked.

"Not as comfortable as yours,by all appearances."

"And our lady,Eva and Blondie the dog?"

"They`ve just arrived separately,and are both well.We have much to discuss-we will arrange further meetings-I am due at the Presidential Palace shortly."

"I will look forward to that,mein Fuhrer-Heil Hitler!"Ele clicked her boot heels as the hunched greying figure with his trademark moustache shaven off climbed back into his limousine.

Modz breathed a deep sigh,turned to Ele and told her:"So you`re back in the BDM- congratulations .Was it really necessary to refer to Eva as `our lady`,as if she was the Virgin Mary?"

"Yes,if we want good relations with him-do you think he`s the real thing or another lookalike?"

"Too hard to tell,but I`ve never met him-you have-what do you think?"

"Evita Peron thinks he`s the real thing-maybe that`s all that`s needed."

"Maybe,"Modz sighed,"let`s go and see the room she`s reserved for us in the Palace."

”Yes,let`s”.Ele answered,and turned towards the jet-black waiting limousine.

ABOUT THE AUTHOR

Dr Paul Camster

https://www.amazon.com/Paul-Camster/e/B004K-DVIRM/ref=dp_byline_cont_pop_ebooks_1

BOOKS BY THIS AUTHOR

Young Nixon Kindle Edition

Grim Kindle Edition

The Gold Tinderbox Kindle Edition

Apocalypse Third Edition Kindle Edition

Ironclad

Apocalypse First Edition

The Caspar Enigma

Crime&Punishment

The Newton Inheritance

Voice Of The Demon

All Time High

The Master Therion

The Messiah Stone

Precoded

Magicians Code

Apocalypse Second Edition

Triple Cross